GW01418860

Published in Great Britain in 2018 by Mascot Media (Norfolk)
for Rosie Andersen.
Email: mascot_media@btinternet.com
Web: www.mascotmedia.co.uk

© 2018 Rosie Andersen. Illustrations © Paul Jackson.

Web: www.aelfwynnbooks.com

Web: www.pauljacksonstory.com

A CIP catalogue record for this book is available from the British Library.

ISBN: 978-1-9998457-9-7

Rosie Andersen has asserted her right under the Copyright, Design and Patents Act, 1988, to be identified as the author of this book.

All rights reserved. No part of this publication may be reproduced, stored in a retrieval system, or transmitted in any form or by any means electronic, electrical, chemical, mechanical, optical, photocopying, recording or otherwise, without the prior written permission of the publisher.

Written by Rosie Andersen. Design and layout by Alan Marshall (Mascot Media). Artwork scanning & image processing by Alan Marshall. Edited and proofreading by Marion Scott Marshall (Mascot Media).

Printed by Swallowtail Print, Drayton Industrial Park,
Taverham Road, Drayton, Norwich, Norfolk NR8 6RL.
Email: contact@swallowtailprint.co.uk
Web: www.swallowtailprint.co.uk

With special thanks to: Lizzi Thistlethwayte, Sonya Farrell, Professor David Cadman, David Truzzi Franconi, Christopher Clark, Sandra Smith, Dr Ian Baillie, Richard Hartley, Mrs Anne Cuddigan and Janine Edge.   **Rosie Andersen**

Translations of the Anglo-Saxon Riddles 'The Storm' and 'The Goose' from **The Exeter Book of Riddles** *by kind permission of Kevin Crossley-Holland (www.kevincrossley-holland.com). Translation of 'Leeches' from* **Saint Aldhelm's Riddles** *by kind permission of A.M. Juster (www.amjuster.net).*

CONTENTS

INTRODUCTION

Stories, whether myths, legends, fables, fairy tales or parables, are common to all cultures. Many adults will still remember with great affection the stories they were told as children and when imaginations were captivated. For contained within these often seemingly simple tales are wisdoms, sophisticated ideas and universal truths that represent values, virtues or principles, and help us live authentic lives.

Ultimately, it is the message contained within the stories that is significant. The reader, whatever their age or gender, being either read to or reading for themselves, will draw whatever is relevant or significant to them for that moment. Very often written in the language of metaphor and symbolism, these stories are multi-layered and shape not only cultural traditions but also our personal beliefs.

*Our daily lives are also made up of stories that are created by us and by others. These give shape, meaning and purpose to our existence as individuals and can, in turn, affect how we interact with others. These stories can be a fusion of positive cultural and family influences and not-so-helpful fabrications of how we want to live our lives or how we want to be seen by others, as in the case of Leof, our young protagonist in **The Lost Key**.*

Here, through his mother's inherited beliefs, fears and insecurities that she projects on to her young and vulnerable son, Leof inherits a story about himself so oppressive that it is in danger of overwhelming him and preventing him from living a happy and fulfilled life. He is completely unsure of his emotions because he doesn't know what part of him is real.

*Containing much analogy, **The Lost Key** is a tale of adventure and fortitude; about the complexities of human nature and our attempts to conquer our demons. With equal importance, it is a story about friendship and the soul connection between the enigmatic characters of Leof and Elswyth.*

ROSIE ANDERSEN

THE LOST KEY

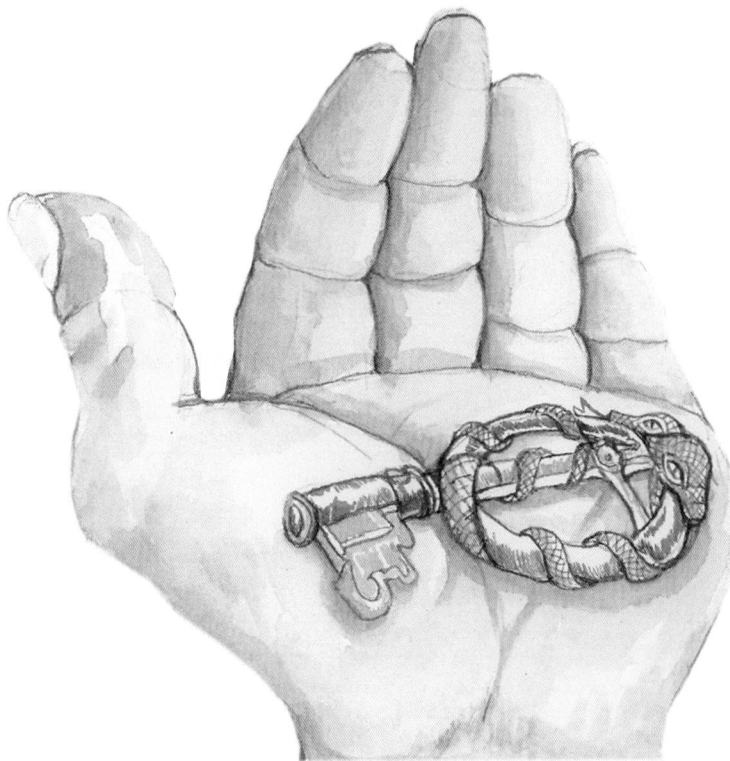

"A tree is known by its fruit; a man by his deeds.
A good deed is never lost; he who sows courtesy reaps friendship,
and he who plants kindness gathers love."

SAINT BASIL

Chapter 1: MYNDA

The tall, solemn elms whispering tales of times past grew in abundance in the flat, green and water-girdled lands of Suthelmeham, where the folk of the South had made their homesteads. Streams of clean, flowing water meandered across the meadows where alder and willow trees flourished on the banks and wetlands. Here, in the Waneforda Hundred, was the small village of Mynda where Leof and his mother, the widow Wilfreda, had come to live. Leof was Wilfreda's only child, his father having been killed by the warring invaders when he was a baby.

Now was a period of relative peace where time passed slowly and both the people and the land breathed with the ever-changing seasons. But this was also an age when life could be harsh, where survival depended upon everyone, both young and old, and where there was a strong sense of cooperation as the villagers worked for the benefit of each other and their communities. When the great spirits of nature blessed the people with benevolence, and the elements were kind, all flourished and prospered. But at other times during the long, cold and dark winters, there could be hunger, illness and even death.

Wilfreda's work was to spin the fleece from the sheep, weaving the yarn to make clothes for herself and her son, and cloth for the village. Since Leof was born, Wilfreda daily thanked the Goddess Frige for her son, praying that he would stay small and young forever so that he would never leave her. Whilst she spun and wove she would sing softly to him:

"Leof, my beloved, you are mine, all mine.
With your hazel eyes and your raven hair,
the sun, the moon and the stars may shine
but never as brightly or as fair.
For you my child are mine, all mine. For you my child are mine."

Wilfreda doted on her son and would tell him how special he was: more special than anyone else, more clever than anyone else, and that he deserved only the very best that life could bring him. He grew strong like his father, with fine features and thick, wavy hair, but Wilfreda, always worrying unnecessarily about Leof's safety, rarely allowed him out to play with the village children. As soon as Leof was old enough, he would have, for an hour each day, lessons from Brother Eadraed, who came from the Priory to teach him to read and write. It was not the normal practice for village children to have formal lessons, but Wilfreda was so determined that her son would excel in learned matters that she eagerly wove cloth for the monks in return for Leof's tuition. Leof, being a solitary child, was quite content to study on his own; and, not knowing any other way, would play happily and purposefully within his mostly silent world.

When the village children reached 10 years of age, they worked in the fields alongside the adults. They tended the crops, looked after the animals, fished, collected herbs, berries, nuts and fungi. They were also expected to gather wood and water. In addition, the boys learnt how to make tools and carve, whilst the girls were taught to sew, spin, weave, cook, make cheese and brew ale. They worked long, hard days from first light to sunset. Wilfreda preferred Leof to tend the goats nearest to their dwelling so she could watch him from the window where she sat with her spindle and loom. Every day at the tye, Leof filled the water troughs and hay nets using a wether goat to pull the cart. He didn't mind this work as he could always return home when he felt tired or uninterested.

Leof was already learning how to take advantage of every situation…

Loving
and well-intentioned as
Wilfreda was, through her possessiveness
she was hampering Leof's chances of growing into
a well-balanced young man; and he, in turn, as a smothered
and spoilt child, was growing into an unpleasant youth who
thought only of himself and his own needs. He had very few friends, the
other children being wary of him as he was often arrogant, full of
self-importance and avoided his fair share of hard work in the fields.

In truth, Leof was fearful of others finding out that he was not as special as his
mother had led him to believe or that he was less clever than he was showing himself to
be. He learnt from a young age that in order to gain attention he would sometimes have
to pretend to be something he wasn't. He learnt that if you were friendly, generous and
helpful, even if you didn't mean it, then folk would like you ~ and Leof, deep-down inside,
always wanted to be liked.

He would fawn, flaunt and flirt to gain the recognition he needed; and at times, genuinely
believing himself to be unfairly treated, he would also tell woebegone stories to whomever
would listen in order to win their sympathy. If he spent too much time with the same
person, he would become bored and irritable in their company and his displeasure
would start to show. As a result, he avoided getting too close to anyone for fear that
he would be seen as something other than the exceptional person he wanted and
believed himself to be. Sometimes when other children or adults criticised
him or questioned his behaviour, the false mask that Leof had created
for himself slipped and the scared, vulnerable child was revealed.
He would then lash out angrily, blaming others for doing
wrong to him.

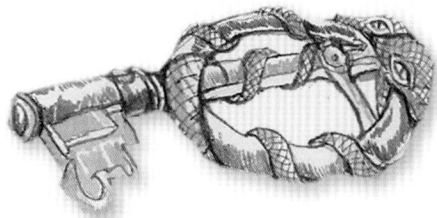

Chapter 2: MASQUERADE

One day, Leof, having left his duties of tending the goats, went to hide under the willows that surrounded the village pond. The large, wise old willows with their pendulous whips hanging like flounced curtains around the fissured bark provided the perfect place to shelter from the hot sun. Here, Leof watched the birds and listened to them singing. This was a place where he felt at peace and at ease, where he could be himself away from the gaze of others who might cause him to become angry.

Leof broke off a whip from the tree and ran it through the water, creating ripples and patterns. Shoals of tiny fish in their hundreds darted in different directions as the soft stem created a disturbance on the surface of the pond. In the sunshine, the movement illuminated the lime-green weed floating in the shallows, causing the light to shift and dance. It was a kaleidoscope of colour that made Leof's vision blur temporarily as he gazed into the water. On looking up, it was through this mirage that Leof saw a tiny, elf-like girl, dressed all in green, appear from amongst the willows as if she were coming out from the trees themselves. He was instantly entranced.

Her name was Elswyth, and she and Leof soon became good friends. They played, they laughed, they walked and talked endlessly, they chased the goats and chickens, they ran across the meadows picking flowers, and swam in the river. In the autumn, they kicked and scattered the falling golden leaves; and when winter came, they made and threw snowballs at each other. At last, Leof had a proper friend, a confidante, and someone he could finally trust. Elswyth, too, was entranced. She admired Leof's knowledge and his seeming confidence. She thought how different he was from the other youths in the village, and she wanted to spend as much time with him as she could.

Although Leof was very fond of Elswyth, his heart, unlike the winter winds, stayed cold to her. He soon realised that because she was so amenable and accommodating, he didn't have to work very hard to gain her attention and could quickly become aloof and indifferent. He worried that the part of him he wanted no one to see would soon be revealed to her. Elswyth, on the other hand, was a true friend to Leof, always showing kindness and patience, supporting him through all his moods and bad behaviour even though she was, at times, punished for witnessing the slipping of his mask.

As time passed, Leof would suffer with angry outbursts when he realised that he actually could not live up to his idea of perfection. He could not bear anyone to challenge him, even though they were very often justified. For Leof, no one could be better than or good enough for him, and as a result the values required for him to live a contented and fulfilled life had become completely distorted.

As the summer months progressed and the crops ripened, very soon everyone in the village would be needed for the harvest to gather the food ready for the colder months ahead. The harvesting, although hard work, was a communal, happy time for everyone. So whilst the weather was kind, the gathering would begin.

At sunrise, with the promise of a hot and humid day ahead, the villagers assembled at the tye – bringing with them their implements and carts. Out in the fields the men worked in even lines cutting the grain with long, wooden-handled scythes, the sharp blades passing in a regular rhythm back and forth through the stalks, producing a ringing tone as the metal hit the brittle stems.

The younger children watched, captivated by the precision of the cutting as the men moved with swiftness and synchronicity across the fields. The speed at which the men scythed created a constant swooshing sound that filled the air, mimicking the wings of swans in flight; and clouds of dust billowed upwards, causing a hazy mist that hung heavy in the still sky.

When it was the turn of the women to begin the reaping, they placed damp cloth over their heads and faces to protect their eyes and breathing. Then the cut crops were raked and stacked into sheaves, the younger children tying the bundles together using strands of wheat. At the heat of day, harvesting stopped whilst the villagers shared bread, cheese and fruit.

Elswyth noticed that Leof was nowhere to be seen; in fact, she hadn't seen him for some while. Leof had slipped off during the morning as the sun rose higher in the sky and the temperature climbed. He was too hot and didn't feel he should be made to work with the others, so he sat under the willows surrounding the pond watching the birds, playing with the water and reading his book that Brother Eadraed had given him.

Whilst leaning over the water looking for fish, Leof saw in the depths a beautiful face that took his breath away. He gasped, for it was the most beautiful face he had ever seen. Leof smiled, the face smiled gently back, he tilted his head, and the face in the water did the same. Leof then raised his hand and waved at the smiling face. He took a sharp intake of breath when the image in the water waved back. He was spellbound and wanted to stay there forever, just watching.

Leof was falling in love with his own reflection

His moment of reverie and silence was abruptly interrupted by Elswyth's voice calling, "Leof, Leof, where are you?" Before he had time to hide further or even think about answering her, she had spotted him. "There you are! People are beginning to notice that you are not at the harvest. You must come back and join the men for the scything."

Leof replied angrily, "Yes, I'll come back, but not for you or because you've asked me to." He sneered, "In fact, I no longer want to be friends with you because I've never really been interested in what you say or do! I have just fallen in love with the most beautiful person imaginable, and you are not clever or lovely enough for me."

Elswyth, although used to Leof's moods, was so shocked by his sudden pronouncement that she was, for that moment, struck speechless. Not knowing what to say, she turned away with tears in her eyes and ran back to the tye and the harvest activities.

Leof continued to go to the pond every day looking for his beloved in the water. Some days he saw the beautiful face, and other times he didn't. He became very despondent, blaming Elswyth for causing his beloved to leave him. So Leof decided that he would punish Elswyth and not speak to her – at least until it suited him to do so again.

Over the winter months Elswyth rarely saw Leof. She was occupied with more indoor activities and helping her parents with the collecting of wood to keep their dwelling warm. Leof continued to work with the goats but avoided Elswyth and the other young villagers. Elswyth tried to be happy but she missed Leof and the times they had spent together very much.

Chapter 3: THE GREEN MAN

As winter turned to spring and the cycle of the seasons continued, the village once more became busy with outdoor activities. There were fields to be ploughed and crops to be sown. Thoughts were also turning to preparations for the very important annual Green Man celebrations.

In the year of their 14th birthdays, the youth within the villages of the Waneforda Hundred were each given a golden key by a mysterious Green Man, a rarely seen creature that lived in the depths of the woods. The Green Man was also to be found in churches where local craftsmen had carved its foliate image in stone and wood. The presentation of the golden keys was to aid the opening of the hearts of the young people to virtues and values that would equip them for their passage into adulthood.

This sacred festival, a rite of passage, attended by all the villagers from the Hundred, was accompanied by great celebrations ~ with maypole dancing and much merrymaking. At the forthcoming ceremony, Leof, along with Elswyth, was to be one of the recipients. Food and drink were prepared, new clothes were made, and anticipation was in the air.

On the first day of May, the young people gathered at the tye dressed in their finest woven garments. Elswyth wore a green dress that had been embroidered with gold thread around the neck and sleeves, and over this she wore a red tunic held by a plaited belt on which hung a goatskin pouch. New leather shoes had been made, and on her head she wore a beautiful garland of spring flowers intricately entwined.

Leof also had new clothes finely made by his mother. His new blue cloak was highly embroidered, too, and around his waist he wore the heavy brown belt that had belonged to his *father. Both Elswyth and Leof, wearing their new garments, all of a sudden looked transformed from awkward youths to young adults.*

In the centre of the tye was a tall birch maypole, adorned at its highest with garlands and blossom, from which hung strips of cloth in many colours. Brother Eadraed and the other monks from the Priory came to play their lyres and bone flutes, and a group of men and women from the village sang, played drums and blew on horns.

As the light started to fade, bonfires were lit and the feasting prepared. The youth began to gather near to the maypole, with the youngest children forming an inner circle nearest to and around the pole; whilst the older children, boys and girls alternately, took up their positions forming an outer circle, each holding one of the coloured ribbons.

As the music began, the younger children, with clasped hands, moved around the maypole; whilst the older group, including Leof and Elswyth, began to dance, slowly and carefully, weaving in and out of each other, the ribbons passing over and under, becoming elaborately intertwined and plaited. The hypnotic boom of the drums gathered pace, and the dancers quickened their step. The singers' voices became louder and, along with the other instruments, produced an other-worldly sound that carried far into the darkening night.

Once the pole had almost been covered with the overlaid cloth, the dancers then retraced their steps to unwind the ribbons. Leof, who wanted to continue with his punishment of Elswyth, was unable to avoid her during the dance, and, although he passed her frequently, he deliberately made no eye contact.

As darkness fell, clouds of red sparks from the bonfires flew into the cooling air whilst the villagers, including the young initiates, gathered around the fires to keep warm. Then, coming across the tye, flares of light could be seen bouncing in the dark and a solemn rumble of beating drums could be heard. As the light and sound grew closer, a group of men emerged from the dark, walking menacingly towards the central bonfire. At the front of this procession, flanked by men with blackened faces and carrying flamed torches, slowly walked the Green Man. He was a daunting sight, huge in stature and completely covered in foliage so that only his eyes were visible.

Once at the central bonfire, the Green Man called each of the young adults to come up, one at a time, to be given their golden key that had been inscribed with a specially chosen symbol. When it was her turn, Elswyth, with reverence, bowing her head in respect, walked up to the Green Man who presented her with her key inscribed with a dove – for, unbeknown to Elswyth, she was to be a peacemaker, a messenger.

Leof was not so respectful. He thought the key-giving ceremony to be foolish, believing that he was above all of this nonsense. However, he went along with it all in order to look favourable, and he received his key that was inscribed with the symbol of a snake, which, unbeknown to Leof, was for his transformation. At the first opportunity, though, Leof tossed it into the hedgerow when no one was looking.

Once all had received their keys, the feasting began with much frivolity taking place until dawn. The next morning, the dark and ominous silhouette of the Raven Hremm could be seen circling above the tye, chuckling and gurgling to himself. Suddenly, the large black bird descended to the ground with speed. It was not prey that attracted him but something sparkling and glowing in the undergrowth. He had found Leof's key. With a sardonic caw he scooped up the key in his beak and flew away into the distance.

Chapter 4: THE QUEST

Over the coming weeks life in Mynda once again returned to its usual routine, with the villagers making the most of the long summer days ahead.

For Leof, this meant a return to his duties of tending the goats and being involved with other communal tasks. He continued to visit the willow pond in search of his beloved, and would dream of the great wealth and admiration he felt he was entitled to. He also dreamt about being somewhere else, somewhere where he didn't have to work with the goats any more.

Leof was becoming exasperated with his lot, and his behaviour grew increasingly disagreeable to others. The village youth avoided him, and he found himself becoming jealous of their happiness and unfolding maturity. "I so want to be like them," Leof bemoaned, as he crossed the tye to stand beneath the birch pole.

The ceremony of the Green Man and his gift were still vivid in Leof's mind. "Perhaps I should not have thrown my key away," he thought. Having desperately searched high and low for this, an unhappy Leof was now beginning to understand its importance. Asking Brother Eadraed about his dilemma, Eadraed earnestly answered, "My child, there is only one solution to your sorrow and that is to go on a quest, a journey, to search for the gifts that your key would have given you."

"But how can I do this?" asked Leof.

Eadraed replied, "You must take this map and travel to all of the places marked, seek out the Green Man who lies hidden within the structure of each of the churches and from whom you will receive guidance that will help you on your journey. I must stress that there can be no compromises and you must follow all instructions precisely in order to reach your goal.

"There will be great challenges and dangers, and you will be tested. Dear Leof, you can no longer pretend; the mask you have created must fall fully away in order for you to change. Have courage, my child."

So, without further delay, Leof collected some belongings: a strong hazel staff for protection; his heavy wool cloak and the ornate, jewelled clasp that had belonged to his father; a goatskin bag in which he placed the map; and around his neck he wore the leather and amber necklet given to him by Elswyth when they had first become friends. And so, with a heavy heart and under the cover of darkness, Leof left the village of Mynda not knowing whether he would ever return.

Many a gathering had taken place in the great communal hall of Mynda where, around the central fire, the villagers assembled to hear tales told of the ghosts, goblins, giants and devils that lurked in the woods, the tracks and ditches. Leof was never sure whether to believe such stories, but for some of the villagers these tales of strange beings were true, with many claiming to have seen them.

Soon Leof would come face to face with his own inner demons!

So it was with some unease that Leof began his journey, sleeping out in the open under
the stars and foraging for fruit and nuts to eat. Occasionally, Leof caught sight of Hremm whose
sinister screeches and cackles unsettled him, disturbing his sleep.

Travelling east along the River Dove where the water had created a shallow valley, Leof walked towards Hangman's
Wood through which he had to pass before reaching the church of Seynt Crost. As he came closer to the wood, Leof shivered
as storm clouds gathered and a chill wind blew. Venturing farther along the path through the trees, a deeper coldness descended,
where no animal sounds or birdsong could be heard. The strange silence felt eerie, and Leof sensed a presence watching him as he
tried to increase the speed of his step in order to pass through the wood as quickly as possible.

Suddenly, Leof caught a glimpse of a sinister and ghostly figure gliding towards him in the dull light. He was rooted to
the spot in fear as the form came closer, dressed in a hooded monk's robe with a rope belt from which hung a noose, its skeletal feet
dangling. There was no face, only a cavernous, black abyss.

The spectre spoke with a deep and grating whisper. "I am Drog of the Weald. This is a place of troubled souls where the sun never
shines. Who is it that passes this way?"

"I am Leof, son of Wilfreda. I am travelling on a quest in order to receive guidance from the wise
Green Men of the Hundred so that I can find my true self. I have been thoughtless and unkind
to many people, only ever thinking about myself."

"So is it empathy and humility you seek?" Drog enquired.

"Yes, I suppose it is!" Leof replied with surprise, having not previously
thought that he might be lacking in any virtues.

Drog continued, "Only if you can solve my riddle will you pass unscathed…"

"Who is so clever and quick-witted as to guess who goads me on my journey when I get up,

angry, at times awesome;

when I roar loudly and rampage over the land, sometimes causing havoc; when I burn houses

and ransack palaces? Smoke rises, ashen over roofs.

There is a din on earth, men die sudden deaths when I shake the forest, the flourishing trees, and fell timber –

I with my roof of water, an avenger driven far and wide by the powers above;

I carry on my back what once covered every man, body and soul submerged together in the water.

Say what conceals me or what I, who bear this burden, am called?"

The phantom rasped, "An answer, quick, an answer – or you will never again see the light of day!" Leof closed his eyes to concentrate. What if he guessed wrongly? He trembled at the thought. Every second seemed like an eternity when, all of a sudden, the skies rumbled a sign. In a moment of clarity, Leof answered:

"It's a storm… the answer is a storm!"

Drog shrieked with rage and fury at the speed of Leof's correct response as he grew immense, hovering over Leof and almost enveloping him. The wind howled and lightning flashed through the spectre's flowing robe and from its outstretched arms; the rain lashed down, soaking Leof to the skin.

Leof cowered beneath Drog's looming presence; and, looking up in horror, he saw his own reflection staring down at him from the hooded blackness. Leof held up his hazel staff and, with one deafening clap of thunder, Drog shrivelled and withered away into the ether, leaving nothing but the noose – which fell to the ground with a thud, clearing the way for Leof to pass.

He quickly picked up the fragment of rope, put it in his bag and ran as fast as he could out of the woods, relieved to be in the light and warmth once again.

Following the map, Leof, having lost track of time, continued to walk for days.
At last he reached a narrow bridge, passing simple headstones, amongst which dog
violets, ivy flowers, roses and honeysuckle leisurely grew. He had arrived at Seynt Crost, and
saw ahead a small timber church. Leof pushed against the heavy door, which creaked open and
he tentatively entered the coolness of the building.

Looking upwards, Leof, expecting the interior to be dark and dreary, was pleasantly surprised by how the
roof was filled with light from the high clerestory windows illuminating the large rood ahead. He recalled
Eadraed's instructions, and slowly walked around the aisles to see if he could spot the elusive Green Man.

All of a sudden, as if out of nowhere, he heard a voice that appeared to bound around the church, coming from
many directions. The words reverberated:

"I am here, I am there, I am everywhere!
I am in the crevices and the hollows, the rafters and the carvings.
I am amongst the tombs, too,
I am peeping out… and watching you!
So find me… if you can!"

Leof rushed around following the voice as it spoke, hoping to catch a glimpse of its master, but the sound moved too quickly. Finally, Leof stopped abruptly at the base of the rood loft stairs as the echo disappeared up the narrow stone steps. Leof, out of breath and dizzy, peered cautiously up ~ and there, looking down at him, was the grimacing face of the Green Man.

"Welcome, Leof, to Seynt Crost," he said, mockingly. "How clever of you to find me. Tell me, why are you here and what is it you want of me?"

Leof spoke nervously, "I am here to receive guidance from you that will help me find my true self. I don't know which part of me is real." Leof continued, "I have often been thoughtless, only ever thinking about myself. I want to be liked but I don't know how to do it in a way that doesn't push people away. I fear being abandoned when it's revealed that I am not who I seem to be."

The Green Man paused to think, then said, "As you have foolishly thrown away your sacred key, your first task is to collect the key-like leaves from the ash trees growing near the beck. These will give you wisdom and insight for your journey. Then you must look for some leaves of borage to give you strength and courage."

With the instructions given, the Green Man vanished into the walls of the church and Leof went outside to search for what he needed. A little while later, with the ash keys and borage leaves safely added to his bag, Leof continued on his way.

After leaving Seynt Crost, Leof turned south and wandered the lanes and paths, making shelter wherever he could. He noticed how beautiful the countryside was and how being out in the open air, amongst the trees and animals, made him feel at ease. He was having plenty of time to reflect on his behaviour towards Elswyth, and he began to feel ashamed.

At home in Mynda, Elswyth, carrying a deep sorrow at Leof's sudden disappearance, visited the willow pond daily in the hope that she would find him once again, sitting quietly reading by the trees.

"Where are you, Leof, where are you…?"

…Elswyth called out in anguish, but a reply never came.

Her solitary figure was often to be seen walking the paths of the Hundred, searching for Leof, but she could never find him and her heart felt broken.

She once asked Brother Eadraed, "Where is Leof; will he ever come home?"

"I know not, my child. Leof has undertaken an important journey; he has many challenges and dangers to face. We must pray for his safe return."

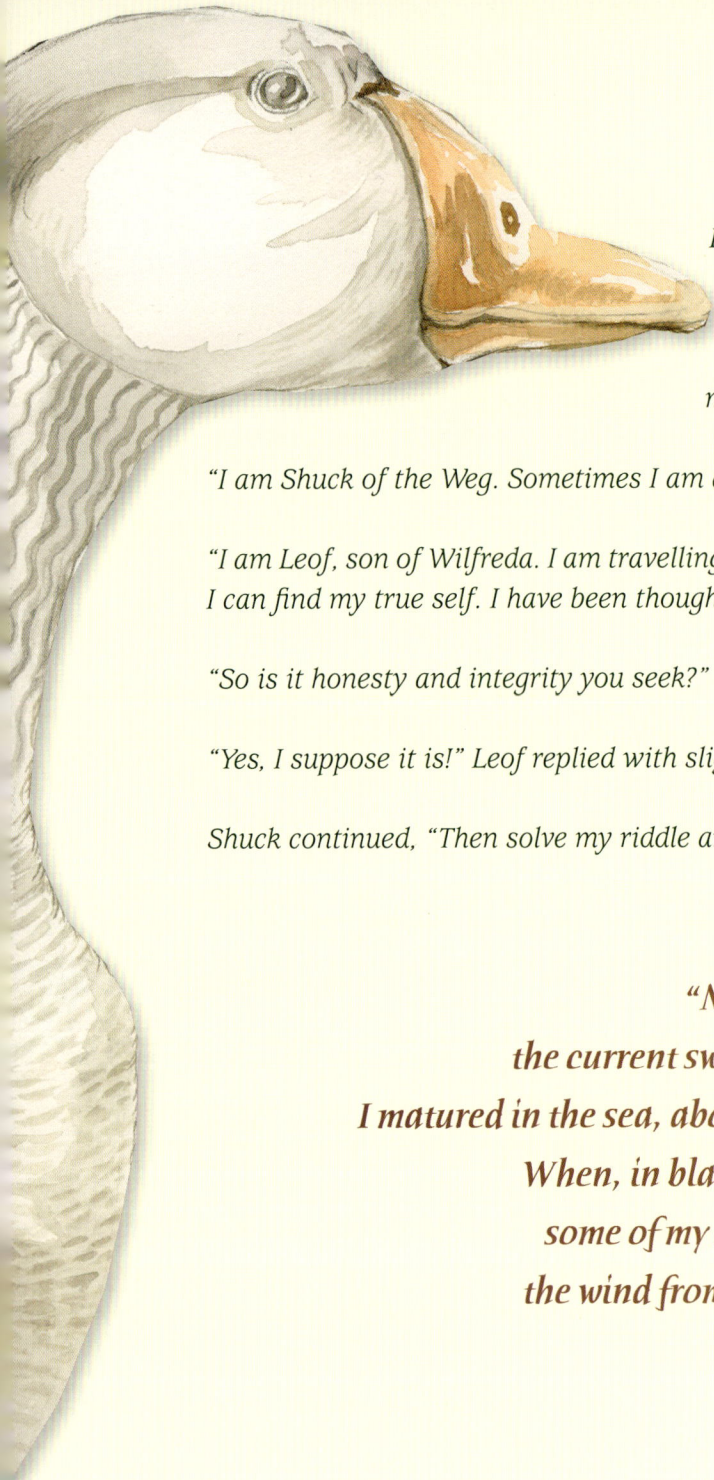

Leof now entered an enclosed track along which grew dense hedgerows. From the thickets, he heard the sounds of geese honking and hissing in a nearby field, their squawks sounding a warning. Unexpectedly, from the impenetrable growth that bounded the path, jumped a grotesque, stout goblin with a large head and bulging eyes. The little man squealed with menace.

"I am Shuck of the Weg. Sometimes I am animal and sometimes I am human. Who is it that passes this way?"

"I am Leof, son of Wilfreda. I am travelling on a quest in order to receive guidance from the wise Green Men of the Hundred so that I can find my true self. I have been thoughtless and unkind to many people, only ever thinking about myself."

"So is it honesty and integrity you seek?" Shuck asked.

"Yes, I suppose it is!" Leof replied with slight bafflement.

Shuck continued, "Then solve my riddle and you may pass unharmed."

"My beak was bound and I was immersed,
the current swept round me as I lay covered by mountain streams;
I matured in the sea, above the milling waves, my body locked to a stray, floating spar.
When, in black garments, I left wave and wood, I was full of life:
some of my clothing was white when the tides of air lifted me,
the wind from the wave, then carried me far over the seal's bath.
Say what I am called?"

As the hideous goblin aggressively punched the air with his axe, Leof was unable to think clearly and answered the riddle rather too hastily. "A duck?" said Leof.

"Wrong, wrong," the goblin shouted, jumping up and down in glee at Leof's incorrect response. "Try again!" he taunted.

Whilst concentrating hard, Leof happened to glance down at his map. There, written on the parchment, was the clue – Waddlegoose Lane! He took a short, sharp intake of breath at this realisation.

"Can you repeat the riddle?" Leof quickly asked, just to make sure.

"You only get it once," Shuck growled.

So, taking a chance, Leof called out:

"A goose… the answer is a goose!"

The little man angrily stamped the ground in frustration at Leof's reply. Then, snorting and spitting, the freakish creature, with his raised axe, lunged towards Leof who held up his hazel staff in defence.

Leof recoiled in fright when he saw his own bejewelled cloak clasp pinned to the changeling's tunic. Before he had time to grasp fully what he was seeing, the goblin had shape-shifted into a Greylag goose, disappearing as quickly as he arrived, back through the dense hedgerow, leaving only the clasp on the ground and a single, dark feather floating slowly down.

Leof, mightily relieved, quickly picked up the clasp and feather and hurried on his way.

Time passed slowly as Leof continued
to visit the seven marked churches shown
on his map, attempting to find the elusive Green
Man who each time played cunning, roguish games
on him. With every encounter, Leof was instructed to
collect nature's gifts from the seasons, including hazel nuts
for wisdom; beech nuts for empathy and patience; rosehips f[or]
compassion; and ivy for friendship – all to aid his transforma[tion]
and which he carefully placed in his goatskin bag along with t[he]
noose, the ornate clasp and his newly found goose feather.

On his travels, Leof fought a swarm of bees in Honeypot Lan[e]
and ran through Snakes Wood in swirling mists. In
torrential rain whilst walking Swiltub Lane, he
stumbled upon a sounder of fierce wild boar;
and in driving snow he shivered over the
Devil's Dyke, all whilst the forbidding
presence of Hremm continued
to circle overhead and
watch him.

Leof was now approaching the Grundle, a deep holloway within which grew tall trees, their gnarled and twisted roots emerging from the banks like distorted limbs that caused the track to become hazardous to pass in places. Ahead, Leof saw what looked to be a watery, flooded area; and, as he approached, he was aware of the overwhelming smell of rotting vegetation. Then the ground began to shake and the surface of the boggy area rippled, then gurgled and burbled. With a horrendous and deafening roar, out of the depths a vast, slime-covered creature arose, its huge body reeking of decay. With the force of the monster's rise, Leof was thrown back on to the ground as if a bolt of lightning had hit him. He scrabbled backwards, desperate to get away, but the monster strode out of the bog, mud and mire dripping from its hideous form, showering Leof with the foul-smelling silt.

"I am Grimm of the Mor," the monster roared. "Who is it that passes this way?"

Leof, shaken to his core, and stumbling over his words, answered, "I am Leof, son of Wilfreda. I have been travelling on a quest to reclaim my true self; to receive guidance from the wise Green Men of the Hundred. I have been thoughtless and unkind to many people, only ever thinking about myself."

"So is it kindness and compassion you seek?" Grimm asked. This time Leof replied with certainty, "Yes, I believe it is!" Grimm bellowed, "Only those who solve my riddle can pass, then will you be able to complete your journey to transformation." Grimm continued:

"Ghostlike, I haunt the filthy pools of mud
For Fortune tagged me with a gory name
While I was gulping mouthfuls of red blood.
I lack bones, arms, both feet, but all the same
I puncture fearful flesh with triformed nips."

"What am I?" thundered Grimm. Leof, struck dumb from fear, couldn't answer. The threatening presence of the monster loomed large. In his desperation to give the correct answer, Leof looked frantically around him for inspiration, for something, anything that might give him a clue. Leof, in a flash, noticed on Grimm's body many blood-sucking leeches. At that moment, and with no further delay, Leof held up his hazel staff and screamed recklessly at the monster:

"Leeches… the answer is leeches."

Grimm howled, for no one had ever passed by his bog
unscathed. His body shuddered from its core, then began to change
shape. Leof watched in terror as Grimm's limbs became one with his huge body,
turning black and gelatinous, undulating from side to side. Leof panicked, for where
the monster's head had been he fleetingly glimpsed a reflection of himself wearing the amber
necklet that Elswyth had given him.

Grimm's face rapidly mutated into a large sucker with sharp teeth protruding; and then, with its hideous
form held high, the creature fell with an unearthly roar back into the depths of the rotting swamp leaving only
the necklet floating on the surface.

Leof, grabbing the necklet and his bag, ran as fast as he could along and out of the Grundle before collapsing from
exhaustion in a small copse of silver birch trees where he fell into a deep sleep.

Chapter 5: HOMECOMING

Leof, having recovered from his terrifying encounters, sat in the warmth of the afternoon sun. Signs of spring were everywhere, with the vibrant calling of birds all around. The hawthorn and blackthorn were in flower, and the bright-green crosiers of young ferns were beginning to unfurl. Leof felt that he, too, was uncoiling like the fern, his true nature beginning to show itself, loosening and softening, releasing his negative traits that had so often hurt others. He picked one of the tight, glossy spirals and put it in his bag. In the breeze that rustled the treetops, he was sure he could hear the voice of Elswyth whispering:

"Where are you, Leof, where are you?"

Through the peaceful, undulating countryside and heading in a westerly direction, Leof walked the narrow lanes towards his final destination, to the impressive Minster at Suthelmeham. He crossed a wide and deep moat over which were four narrow causeways forming a perfect cross. Leof crept into the quiet chapel and was struck by the beauty of the place and how peaceful it made him feel. There was little light inside except that coming from the lighted candles and two small round windows on the west wall. He passed a stone partition that divided the nave into two parts, and whilst walking towards the semi-circular apse he heard the voice of the Green Man:

"I am here, I am there, within and without,
I am in all that you see and do.
I am in the wood, the stone, the crevices, the hollows, and the corners.
I am in the trusses, the rafters, the porches and the carvings.
I am in the blades of grass and amongst the tombs too.
I am peeping out… and watching you… so find me if you can!"

Leof looked carefully around the chapel when he spied an eye peering at him through a little hole in the bench end of a pew, around which were carved fronds of foliage.

"Welcome, Leof, to Suthelmeham Minster," the Green Man spoke. "You have done very well, and I congratulate you for having come this far on your journey." He continued, "Your key was taken by the Raven Hremm who has been your companion, watching over you on your journey. Through the successful completion of all your challenges, the dark has been transformed into the light. You may now return to Mynda."

The magic of Leof's quest was plainly becoming clear. He had travelled far on a journey that initially he did not feel he needed. He left the village as a conceited youth, full of his own importance, using people to boost his self-worth but knowing deep down inside that he was walking on a knife edge and that the mask he had created could fall at any time.

How blind and foolish he had been, and he was determined to make amends

On this quest Leof had been tested by many perils, each time discovering aspects of himself that surprised him. He was at last acquiring the virtues and values that would equip him for his life ahead and that would enable him to live a contented life in harmony with others.

Feeling very humbled, Leof thanked the Green Man and left the chapel, stepping out into the warmth of the dappled sunshine. He looked overhead and noticed that there was no longer any sign of Hremm but instead hovered a beautiful white dove that was singing to him. In the song he was sure he could hear Elswyth's mournful cry:

"Where are you, Leof, where are you?"

Leof hurriedly turned north, walking the tracks to return to Mynda, eager to see his home again and particularly Elswyth. He held tightly to his goatskin bag that contained the precious items he had collected. These he would give to Elswyth.

The last part of Leof's quest was tranquil as he passed familiar landmarks – the tall elms that bordered the river where he and Elswyth swam, the clusters of dwellings, the cultivated fields, the copses and the willow pond. As Leof neared the village, he met Brother Eadraed and was keen to tell him of his adventures and how all the obstacles he had met had changed him.

Eadraed listened patiently; and, although very pleased to see Leof, was strangely solemn and appeared troubled. They shared some mead before Eadraed finally spoke of his unease and sadness.

"We rarely set out on a journey knowing every twist and turn."

"Yes, I understand that now," Leof replied. "I could never have foreseen the experiences I came face to face with."

Eadraed continued, "We all have our own journeys to undertake, hurdles to overcome and demons to slay. I need you to come with me, Leof; I have something to show you."

As Eadraed guided him along the path to the Priory, Leof looked at Eadraed enquiringly. "Is there more for me to learn on this quest?"

Eadraed, with great kindness, spoke gently, "You have done very well, my son, your transformation is complete. But, sadly, you are too late to see Elswyth; she will not be able to share in your victory."

He took Leof by the arm and led him to the small graveyard next to the Priory and there, at the edge, in a quiet, shaded spot, was Elswyth's grave, the inscription on her stone reading:

Here lies gentle Elswyth, Elf of the Willows

In disbelief and shock, Leof cried out, "But why, why did she die? Now, I am unable to tell her how much she meant to me and how sorry I am for being so unkind."

"She was sorrowfully silent in the last days," Eadraed explained, as best he could. "And when she did speak, she spoke only of you, Leof. The heart is a strange thing; it sees much that is hidden to the eye. Sweet Elswyth loved you above all things, hoping that one day you would return and become the man she knew you could be. Her heart, once so full of love and joy, became heavy with melancholy. Simply, her heart was broken in losing you."

Leof, in his grief, sat next to the headstone whilst Eadraed left him alone with his thoughts. Through his tears, Leof looked upwards and there the white dove hovered, flying down to alight on Elswyth's grave.

"Here I am." Leof whispered, "here I am."

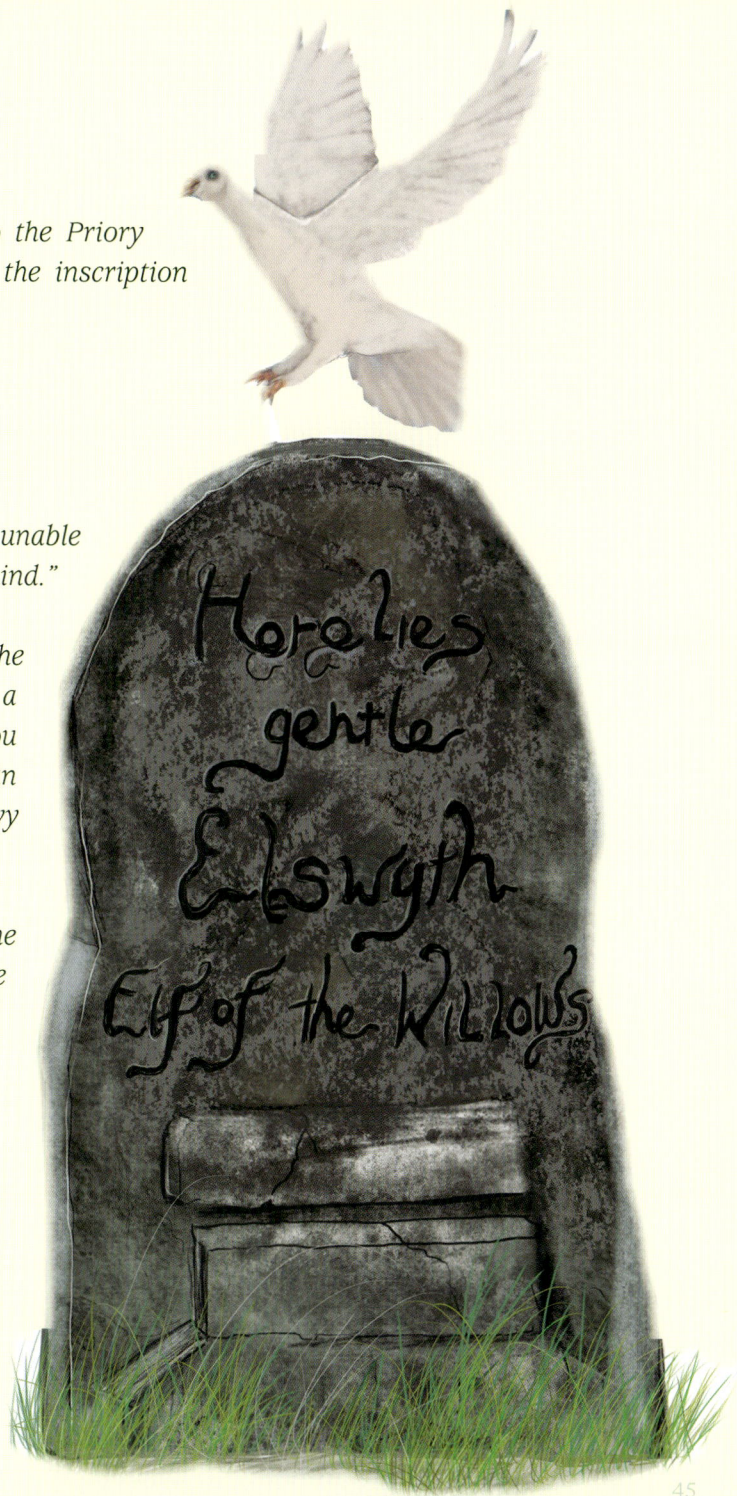

To this day, a dove is always to be seen here. And every year at this resting place, on the day Leof returned from his quest, there grows a single and beautiful snake's head fritillary, marking the spot where Hremm discarded Leof's snake-inscribed key.

"You cannot do a kindness too soon, for you never know how soon it will be too late."

RALPH WALDO EMERSON

GLOSSARY

Leof	'Beloved'
Elswyth	'Elf from the willow trees'
Eadraed	'Blessed counsel'
Wilfreda	'Desiring peace'
Hremm	'Raven'
Shuck	'Witch/devil'
Weg	'Path/track'
Drog	'Ghost/phantom'
Weald	'Wood/forest'
Grimm	'Fierce'
Mor	'Bog'
Green Man	A folklore figure, a symbol of life and nature
Frige	Goddess of love, children and households
Mynda	The village of Mendham in Suffolk
Suthelmeham	South Elmham in Suffolk
Holloway	A sunken lane or track. The name derives from the Old English "hola weg", a sunken road.
Hundred	An area of land encompassing one hundred 'hides' or households
Tye	Village green
Waneforda	An area in Suffolk relating to the River Waveney
Rood	Cross/crucifix
Clerestory	A large window or series of small windows along the top of a structure's wall, usually at or near the roof line
Apse	A semi-circular recess
Grundle	A deep, hollow way with steep banks: the name is unique to East Anglia
Wether goat	A castrated goat